Friends

Margaret K. McElderry Books

Margaret K. McElderry Books
An imprint of Simon & Schuster Children's Publishing Division
1230 Avenue of the Americas, New York, New York 10020
Manufactured in China
Published originally under the title: *Freunde* by Helme Heine by Gertraud Middelhauve Verlag, Köln
Library of Congress catalog card number: 82-45313. ISBN 978-0-689-50256-9

16 18 20 19 17
0515 SCP

Friends

written and illustrated by
Helme Heine

Every morning, when Charlie Rooster strutted into the barn
to wake the other animals, Johnny Mouse and fat Percy went
with him to help. "Good friends always stick together,"
they said. When this job was done, they wheeled their bicycle
out of the barn and set off for their morning ride.

They could ride down the roughest paths and up the steepest cliffs.

No curve was too sharp for them and their bicycle. No puddle was deep enough to stop them.

One day, they played a game of hide-and-seek
by the village pond.

They sailed out on the open water, and as the
day went on, they felt very brave and bold.
They conquered the village pond!

But hunger finally sent them back to the shore.

First they tried to catch a fish. But their stomachs rumbled so loudly that they frightened all the fish away.

Then they went looking for cherries. They shared them: some for Johnny Mouse, some for Charlie Rooster, and twice as many for fat Percy.

Johnny Mouse didn't mind, but Charlie Rooster complained. He said it was unfair. So they gave him the cherry stones. "Friends are always fair," they said.

They ate so many cherries that they all got
stomachaches and had to sit down for a while
before they started back.

As evening fell and the shadows grew longer

they bicycled home.

Behind the henhouse, near the water barrel, they swore to be friends forever.

"Good friends always stick together," they said.

They decided to spend the night in Johnny Mouse's house. But Charlie Rooster got stuck in the doorway.

Then fat Percy invited them to spend the night with him; but Johnny Mouse said he didn't want to sleep in a pigsty.

Finally, Charlie Rooster suggested sleeping in the henhouse. They tried to rest on a perch high above the ground . . .

but it broke. So, sadly, they said good night to each other and went to their own beds. "Sometimes good friends can't be together," they said.

But that night they dreamed about each other, the way true friends do.